ORi's Stars

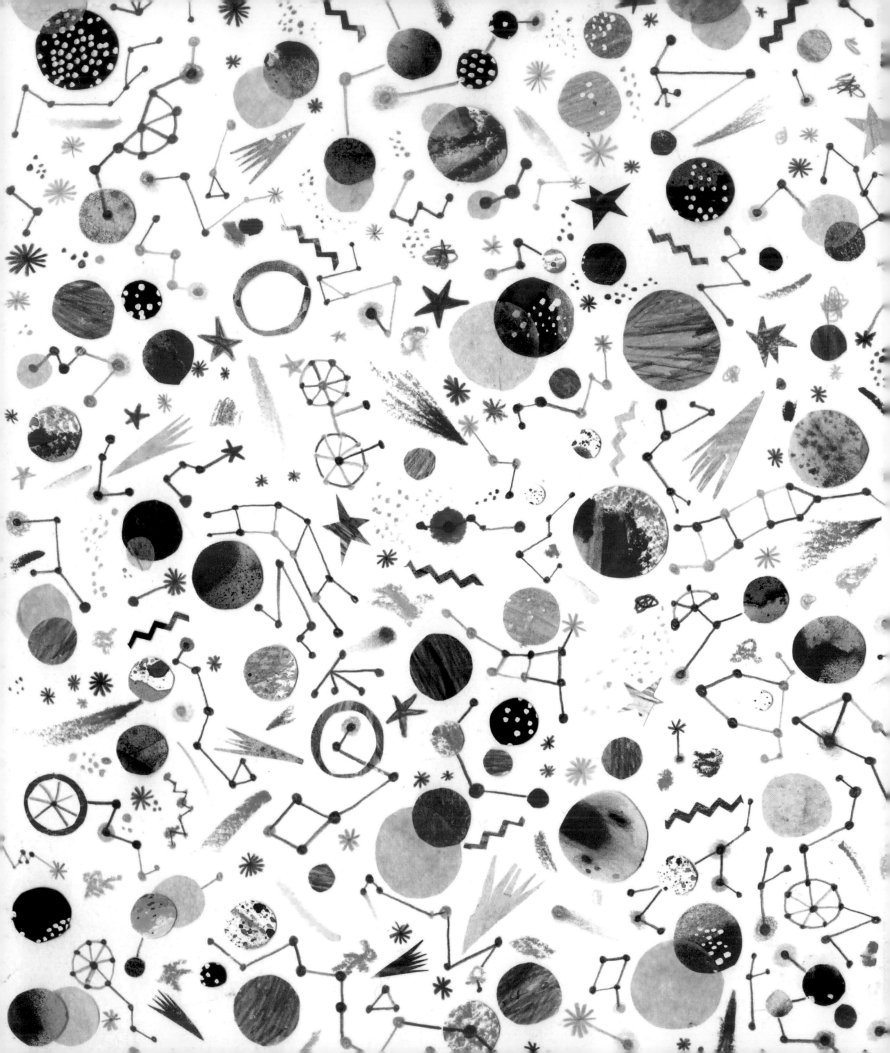

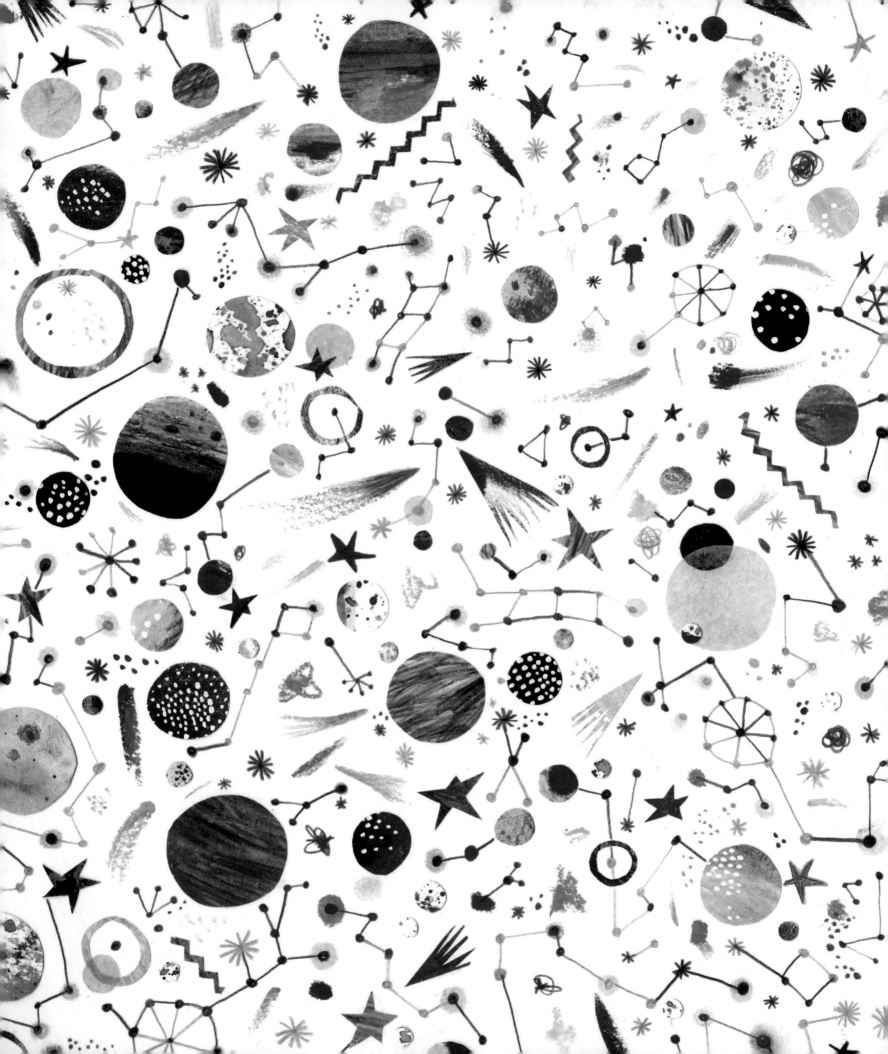

For two new stars, Týna and Ema.

SIMON & SCHUSTER
First published in Great Britain in 2020 by Simon & Schuster UK Ltd
1st Floor, 222 Gray's Inn Road, London, WC1X 8HB • A CBS Company
Text and illustrations copyright © 2020 Kristyna Litten • The right of Kristyna Litten
to be identified as the author and illustrator of this work has been asserted by her in
accordance with the Copyright, Designs and Patents Act, 1988 • All rights reserved,
including the right of reproduction in whole or in part in any form • A CIP catalogue
record for this book is available from the British Library upon request.
978-1-4711-8006-4 (HB) • 978-1-4711-8005-7 (PB) • 978-1-4711-8004-0 (eBook)
Printed in China • 10 9 8 7 6 5 4 3 2 1

ORi's Stars

KRiSTYNA LiTTEN

SIMON & SCHUSTER
London   New York   Sydney   Toronto   New Delhi

Once, there was a something,
who lived somewhere,
who was special somehow.
That something called herself Ori.

She had been lonely in the dark for
longer than she could remember.

Until one day everything changed . . .

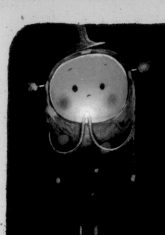

Ori was rubbing her hands
together to keep warm,
when a tiny flicker appeared.

Ori was astonished.
What could it be?

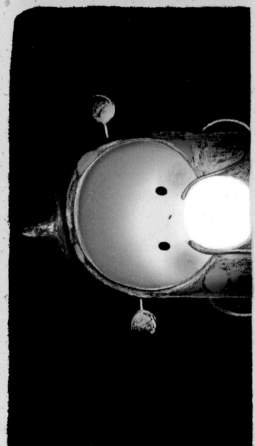

She rolled it from one hand to the other.
It shimmered in the darkness.
Ori couldn't believe she had made
something so beautiful. She called it STAR.

Then she made another . . . and another . . . and another!
The sky around her began to light up.

Suddenly, Ori caught a glimpse
of something in the distance.

It was coming towards her,

nearer and nearer.

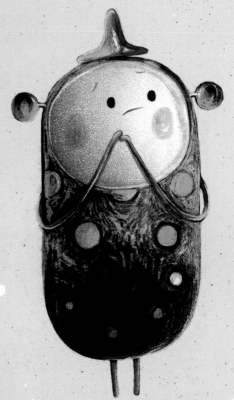

Then with a swish . . .

it was HERE.

Slowly, it reached towards one of Ori's precious stars . . .

"Please don't do that!" Ori gasped.

"I'm sorry," whispered the thing. "Please, could you show me how to make one of my own? I've never seen anything so wonderful."

Ori smiled. Step by step, she showed the thing (whose name was Bella) how to make a star.

And when their star was done . . . Ori was amazed!
It was bigger and brighter than any of the stars
she'd made before.

Just then, as if from
nowhere, a little
voice said . . .

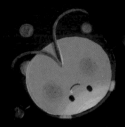

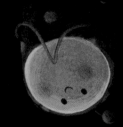

"Can you show me too?"
"Me three!" came another voice.

"And me four."
One by one, more things
stepped out from the dark.
"PLEASE!" they begged.

Soon they were all making stars of their own.

"I'm so glad I found you," said Vega.

"I never knew there was anyone out here," replied Nova.

"This is so much fun," giggled Luna.

Ori's belly fluttered as all sorts of colours
and shapes began to appear across the sky.

As they hopped,

whizzed down curly slides

and burst through
thick clouds

Ori realised she didn't feel
lonely any more and that,
together, they could make
ANYTHING they imagined.

In fact, they were having so much
fun, that before they knew it . . .

there were stars
EVERYWHERE.

Bella even used some of the stars to make a bike!

They peddled round and round
and up, up, up, but all of a sudden . . .

. . . they found themselves in the dark once more.
And Ori realised just how enormous the sky really was.

"There might be others," she whispered, "as lonely
as we were. We've got to help them."

"But how?" said Bella.

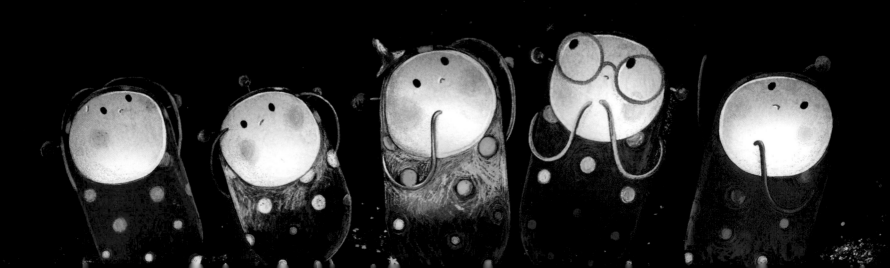

Ori had an idea, but the thought alone made her belly ache. The friends must go their separate ways and spread their light far and wide.

The others were unsure, but Ori knew there was no other way.

"We need to show EVERYONE how to make stars.
If we fill the sky, no one will EVER be alone in the dark again."

Ori's friends understood.
They gave each other one last hug.

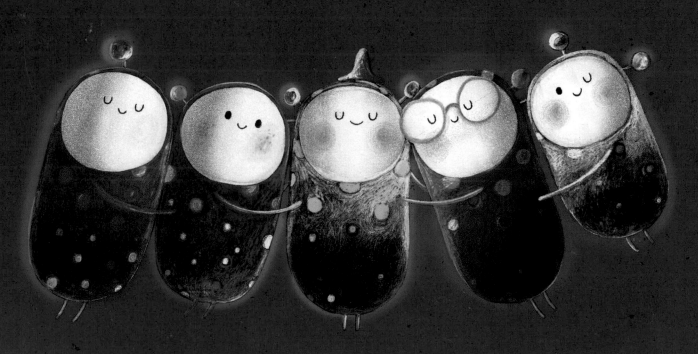

So Luna whizzed east,
Vega whooshed west,

Nova zoomed north and
Bella darted off to the south . . .

. . . until they were no longer in sight.

Ori began slowly pedalling,
making stars as she went.

When she had finished her stars, she suddenly felt quite alone.
There was no one here to share her creations with.

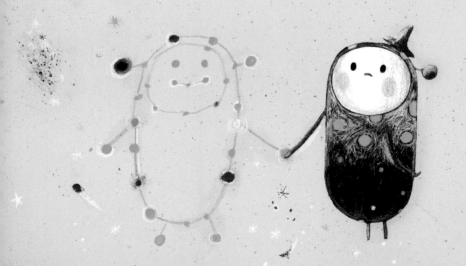

After a long, long time, a teeniest,
tiniest twinkle appeared in the distance.

And then another,

and another . . .

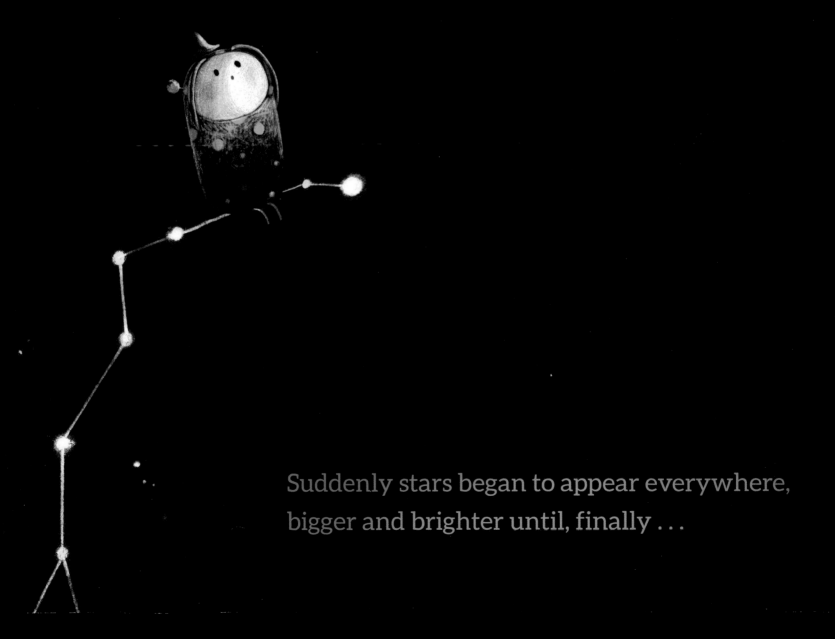

Suddenly stars began to appear everywhere,
bigger and brighter until, finally . . .

...the sky was
filled with stars.

And from that day on,
Ori never felt lonely again.

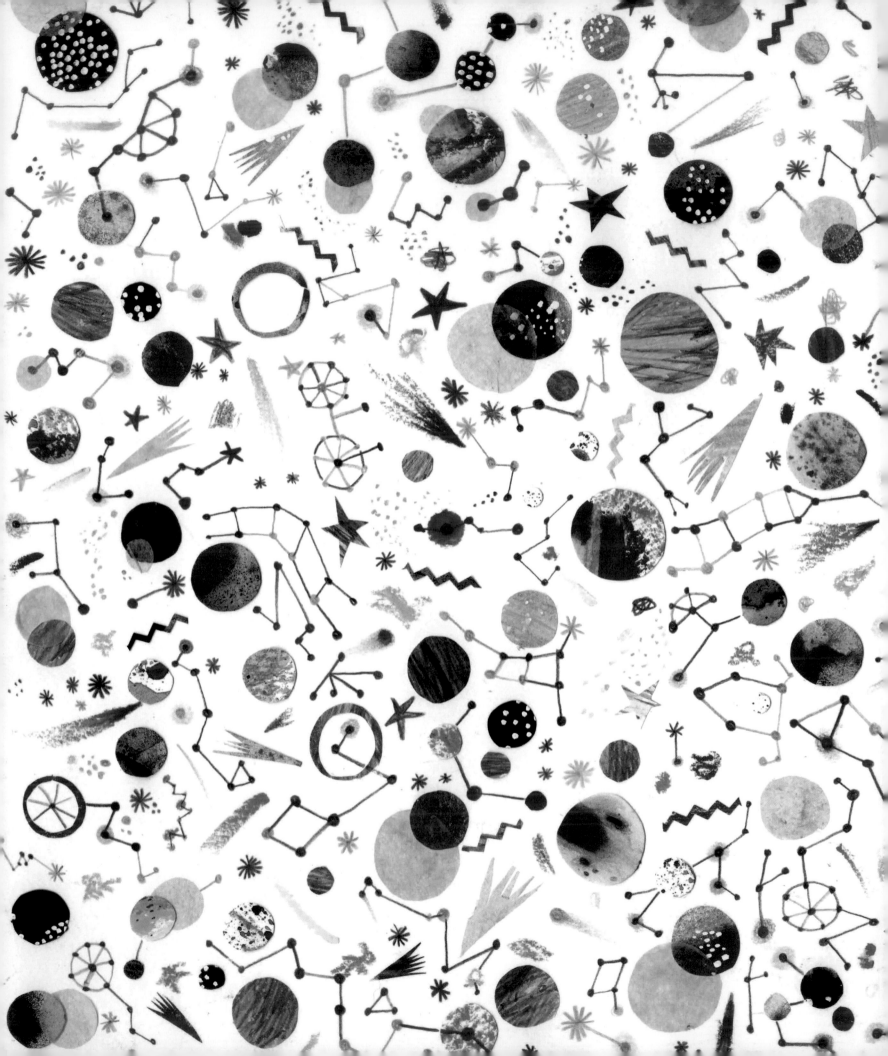

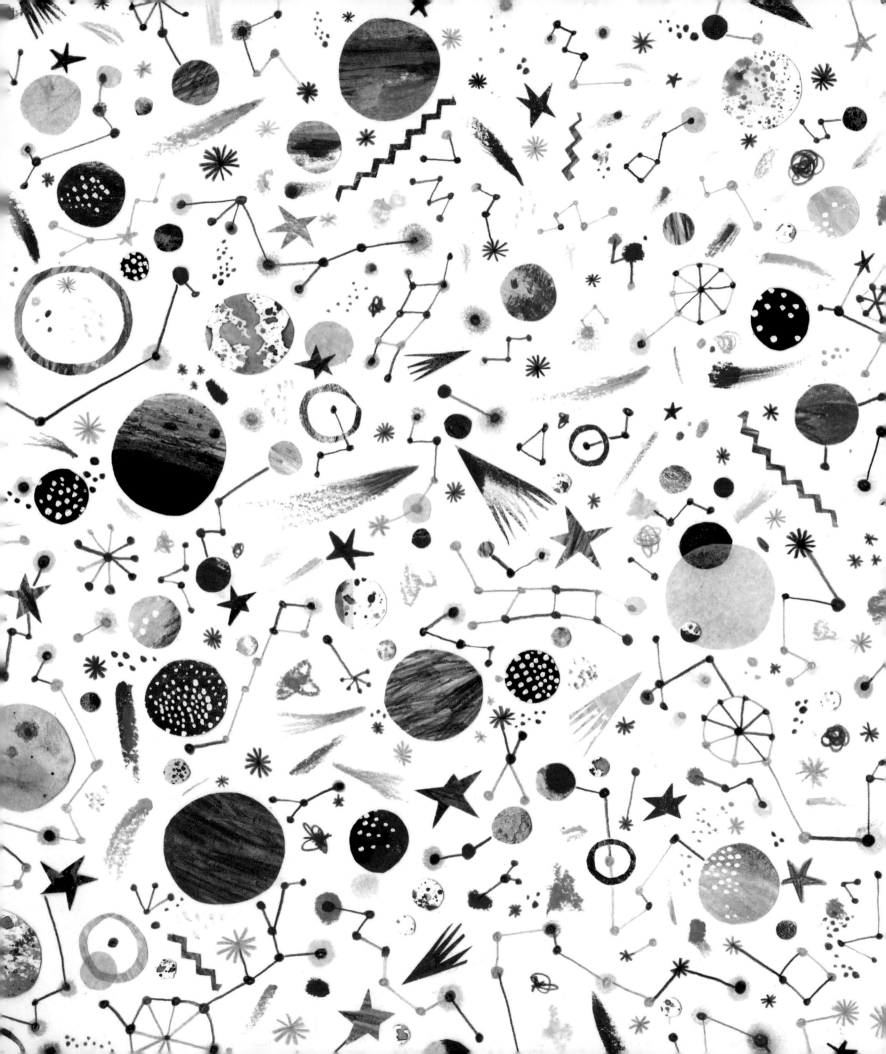